WE are ALL Different, But WE are ALL the Same

The Tails of Nellie Goldie Gray

Tina Sweeney

Balboa Press books may be ordered through booksellers or by contacting:

Balboa Press
A Division of Hay House
1663 Liberty Drive
Bloomington, IN 47403
www.balboapress.com
844-682-1282

Because of the dynamic nature of the Internet, any web addresses or links contained in this book may have changed since publication and may no longer be valid. The views expressed in this work are solely those of the author and do not necessarily reflect the views of the publisher, and the publisher hereby disclaims any responsibility for them.

Any people depicted in stock imagery provided by Getty Images are models, and such images are being used for illustrative purposes only.
Certain stock imagery © Getty Images.

Library of Congress Control Number: 2021923401

ISBN: 978-1-9822-7765-9 (sc)
ISBN: 979-8-7652-3735-9 (hc)
ISBN: 978-1-9822-7764-2 (e)

Print information available on the last page.

Balboa Press rev. date: 11/30/2022

Dedication:

To my profoundly bright and beautiful daughters, Nichole Marie & Jordan Michelle,

Thank you for the infinite inspiration received, by our sharing, in the gifts of music, art and animals! As children you walked with Nellie, always inviting and inspiring everyone with the magic of love!

In admiration of your leadership and life-long examples of hope, acceptance and equality which continue to shine brightly today! You two ARE my greatest blessings!

And to our fuzzurati, Nellie Goldie Gray, thank you for your pure displays of devotion, unconditional love and acceptance you give to ALL creatures on our planet! Forever reminding us - "We are ALL different, but WE are ALL the same!"

With gratitude and immense love,

Mom

This is the Tail of Nellie Goldie Gray,
and how she gives her love away,
unto every creature great and small.
Quiet or loud, Nellie accepts them ALL!

Nellie was born one cold winter day,
on the North American continent, in the USA.
She is from out west, known as the golden coast of fun,
her coat is also golden and glistens in the sun!

She is the last to arrive in the puppy playpen,
with her brothers and sisters they numbered ten.
Nellie is the smallest pup, and when they call her the runt,
she sighs a little grunt!

Nellie also has an odd tail that spins 'round and 'round,
while making a funny swooshing sound!
Although, the other pups certainly try their best,
Nellie always feels they are giving her a test
because her tail is quite different from ALL the rest.

Nellie thinks, "Why do they want my tail wagging to change,
is it because they think it's quite strange?"
Then she heard the people say, "We are worried about finding a
home for this funny tailed pup;
she is so cute and tiny she fits in a teacup!"

Nellie sees the love in their eyes.
But she wonders, "Will I be accepted with my funny swooshing tail
and smaller size?"

Even though Nellie is young she has HOPE!
She is thoughtful and quite wise
as she begins to realize –
"WE are ALL different, but WE are ALL the same!"

3

The puppies grew and grew, and one by one were adopted and taken away,
off to new homes to live, love and play!
Nellie thought to herself, first there were ten, nine and then eight.
She began to wonder if it might be too late.
Now the seven remaining pups played all afternoon,
In the evening three more went out the door, leaving only four.

But Nellie and the three others did not mope.
They bounced and flounced about as they had HOPE!
The next day the sky was gray,
and two more puppies went on their merry way.

Alas, Nellie and her brother felt a little blue,
as now they are the only two in unison they barked, "Boo- hoo!"
Sadly her last puppy brother, Mike, also left the play pen,
leaving behind Nellie, alone without a friend.

Just as she was about to give up,
Nellie heard some exciting voices and her ears perked up!
She was able to cope because she was holding on to HOPE!

Then entered four people filled with joy that Nellie could see!
They were excited to bring a puppy into their family.
Nellie asks herself, "Could it be me?"

The little girls were also small, you see,
only two and five and beaming with glee!
The older girl, called Nikki, exclaimed, "Oh, this is the one –
the puppy I saw in my dreams last night!"
Her little sister, Jordan, screamed with delight,
and so the Tails of Nellie Goldie Gray began that very special day!

Even though Nellie is the runt, a tiny little hound,
and she has an odd tail that goes 'round and 'round
while making a funny swooshing sound,
Nellie is valued, cherished and welcomed inside –
into their hearts, their home and their lives!

Happily, Nellie exclaimed,
"We are ALL different, but WE are ALL the same!"

Nellie grows and grows and loves to explore,
she likes to meet new dogs and make friends galore!
Each and every day she always greets
the dogs and people on the streets.
She becomes known about town as the dog that's never down.
At the park, the beach or in the snow,
in fact, everywhere Nellie would go,
others would notice her odd tail goes 'round and 'round,
and makes that funny swooshing sound!

She continues to ponder if others would accept her this way,
but because Nellie has HOPE and is brave,
she ventures out to find a friend to play!

Much to Nellie's surprise, she discovers most dogs do not look alike,
nor do they resemble her puppy brother Mike.
She is excited yet a little afraid,
Nellie is curious as to what difference this made.

8

She began to discover, life is fun, just like a game -
"WE are ALL different, but WE are ALL the same!"

So she took a journey to the park before it got dark.
As Nellie sat there, under a tree,
she met a tiny dog and thought to herself,
this puppy looks nothing like me.

"My name is Bitsy," said the itsy pup.
She was only inches off the ground, but acting rather tough.
To build this friendship, acceptance and compassion
will be enough!

"Do you like to run a race or play chase?" asked Nellie.
"Yes, I do," Bitsy replied, "May my cousins, Roxy
and Herbie join in the fun too?"
These pups hail from the country of Mexico,
on the continent of North America,
they are ALL the same breed and traveled here with speed!

Just then, Nellie heard a lot of commotion,
but she couldn't see a thing!
Then she saw some motion and had a little notion.

A song made up of high-pitched barks and funny howls filled the air.
Nellie questions, "These silly sounds must come from somewhere?"
As she searched for the source of this noise in the park,
Nellie let out a big bark, and HOPE grew within her heart!

Low and behold, way down by her feet,
were two tiny dogs barking with a beat.
"Hola! We come from Mexico, and we like to sing, growl and howl.
Don't think we are afraid because we shiver,
as this is just our funny quiver.
We have buggy eyes, and we are really brave
and mighty for our size!"

Happily, these four new friends shared a tail-wagging good time!
When the day came to an end,
Nellie said to them, "Thank you for being my friend.
I appreciate sharing your music, the time to play
and most importantly, you ALL accepting me today!"

Nellie, Roxy, Herbie and Bitsy in unison sang,
"I see, you see, and we ALL agree -
"WE are ALL different, but WE are ALL the same!"

Two curious, smaller fluffy dogs, approached Nellie along her way
on this amazing day!
While frolicking by the sea wondered she,
"Would they like to play frisbee with me?"
Although they are stout and thick –
these two can really jump and kick.
As they were coming ashore – Nellie decided to help with an oar.

Now Lili and Angus are quiet proper you see,
they have shaggy fur and funny accents
and don't look or sound like Nellie.
Fluffy and all white, short in height, but strong in might.
These two new friends came from far across the Atlantic sea,
from a little isle in Europe, called Scotland, where HOPE is free!

These rambunctious terriers said to Nellie, "Hello, pip-pip Cheerio!
We are not the same size or the same color as you,
but we like to run and fetch and play frisbee too!"

These three new friends played the day away and laughed as they exclaimed -
"WE are ALL different, but WE are ALL the same!"

Now there came along a giant creature that looked a little scary
and wasn't very hairy.
"Kengan (which means *Hello*), my name is Otis," he said to Nellie.
He comes from a beautiful place called Zimbabwe,
on the African continent, which is far, far away.
Otis is very big, he likes to dig and then go running on the bridge.
Nellie noticed, on his back, he has an interesting ridge.

Otis explains, "In Africa there are many amazing animals
and it is very hot!
Don't be afraid, or think I am angry when my ridge stands up –
As I assure you I am not."

Because he thinks he is the dude,
Otis would peek about and then sneak all the food.
He loves to eat while standing up on his feet
and dancing to the beat.
Otis wants to eat everything in sight,
and he sometimes gives others quite a fright.
So big and crazy he would take the pizza from Miss Daisy.

Nellie thinks to herself – he can't be a dog like me.
He is so big he must be a horse – like I've seen on TV.
"I am Simba-Otis, lion tamer and protector of people," said he.
"I am not horse of course, nor am I a frog. I am just a hungry dog!"

He went on to say, "We both love pizza, dogs and people too –
after all, I am very much like you!
Although, I am big and strong –
I am also meek and gentle and just want to belong!"
Otis has HOPE that all will learn to accept one another;
to walk paw in paw like a sister and a brother!"

Much to their surprise, together they realize –
"We are ALL different, but WE are ALL the same!"

21

The next day, on the prarie, Nellie met a multicolored dog
with bright blue eyes. She thinks he looks quite wise.
Nellie had never met a dog with eyes of blue, and a furry coat,
with so many patterns and various colors in hue.

She was very interested and then he said,
"I came to America on a boat,
and I see you are looking at my colorful coat."
He had sailed over from a place called, *the land down under*,
and Nellie was filled with wonder.

"Good day mate – my name is Aussie, and I come from the continent
of Australia, can we have a play date?"
Aussie explained, "For my work I chase cows all day,
I like it so much, for me it's like play!
My coat is multi-colored so I blend in with the grass and trees –
I protect my herd from many predators and bees!"

So the two new friends began a game of chase,
and forgot they were each from a different place –
they both had HOPE for peace on earth and in space!

Nellie had made another friend,
from yet another continent far across our planet.
She also learned a few new words, such as Aussie and mate,
so she said, "Gee mate, this is great!"
Together they discovered – for peace on earth - it's not too late!

She and Aussie barked joyfully while running to the gate -
"WE are ALL different, but WE are ALL the same!"

On this cold and snowy winter day,
Nellie went to the mountains to frolic and play!
There she saw a dog that looked very serious,
and the markings on her face were quite mysterious.
Nellie really wanted to experience this icy fun,
so she put aside her fear and joined in the run!
"Hello my friend, my name is Suzie and
I come from the South Pole where it is very cold,
my continent is called Antartica and I am very bold!
My eyes look like blue ice and I am very nice!"

Nellie is fascinated as this new acquaintance explained,
"We are Huskies and we travel with speed,
we bring medicine and food to those in need.
I am happy to help and be of service,
so please don't be nervous!
For fun, my breed likes to work, sled and ski,"
Anook-Suzie asked Nellie, "Would you like to try with me?"
These two ventured throughout their day,
helping others along the way!

Learning together even when things are unfamiliar and feel strange,
look further and search for HOPE in the mountains and on the range.
Echoing their message of love - a little red cardinal chirped in a tree,
filling the air with a song of glee!

Nellie and Suzie made snow angels, and shared a soda-pop
as they shouted from the mountain top —
"WE are ALL different, but WE are ALL the same!"

25

It was a magical starry eve, at the beach.
Nellie saw a big, mighty thing —
running about and making the sand fling.
This dog looks different too,
with short square ears and eyes sparkling at you.
She is also very tall and playing with a soccer ball.
Nellie felt the sand and sun, and saw the chance to have some fun!

"Hola, buenas noches, my name is Marta and I am a DOGO," said
this big dog. I come from the continent of South America;
the beautiful country of Argentina where I am a ballerina."

"Others stare at me because I am strong and my legs are very long.
I also have a peculiar bark,
which can be quite alarming — especially in the dark!"
Despite her intimidating size and scary yelp,
Marta was very nice and always willing to help!
Marta said to Nellie, "This might be a shocker,
in my country, we enjoy playing soccer.
We love to eat a mango and dance the tango,
throughout the night — under the Junie Moonlight!"

Nellie thinks to herself once again, "We look nothing alike,
and we come from distant places, but we have HOPE
in all good things and see love in all faces!"

Together, under the moon and stars, they danced and sang -
"WE are ALL different, but WE are ALL the same!"

One spring day Nellie went to the fair.
She was so excited to meet lots of dogs there.
Nellie noticed an odd trio of friends one might not suspect.
They came all the way from the continent of Asia
and have the utmost respect.

The biggest is named Chow-Ming.
the medium sized, called Pugsley likes to sing.
The smallest of the three is Fantasia.
They came from China, to be precise.
somehow they got lost which wasn't so nice!
These three friends were running around scared,
But to help one another, whatever they had they shared.

Chow-Ming is very big and his beautiful coat is black and shiny,
he has lots of wrinkles and his bright brown eyes are tiny.
He is friendly and very strong and helps others to get along.
Sometimes it's hard to tell if he is sad or mad,
but don't be scared, Chow-Ming is very happy and glad!

Far away from the east part of China, on the continent of Asia,
There came this little "kind of funny" pup, her name is Fantasia.
She has no hair, except for a tiny bit on her head, feet and tail.
She is so dainty and petite she can dance on a nail!

The medium sized friend of this trio also has wrinkles
and big brown eyes, he is very fast and hardy —
Pugsley is always the life of the party!
With tan and black fur, and a round face too,
Pugsley makes a funny grunting sound while singing for you.
He just wants to get attention and play,
Pugsley hopes to make a new friend this fine day!

"Wow!" Nellie said to them, "We speak so differently
and sometimes it's hard for us to understand one another,
but with time and understanding,
we realize we are ALL a sister or a brother!"

So these new friends were patient, accepting and giving.
They were not afraid to share so they can all enjoy living!
Discovering they have the dreams
for world peace and belonging under the moon beams!

These four new friends shouted from the ride with pride-
"WE are ALL different, but WE are ALL the same!"

Looking out as the rain danced upon the window pane,
Nellie, without a friend to play, was trying to keep her tears at bay.
She is hoping to find a playmate on this wintry day!

Nellie was a little sad and down,
so she thought it would be exciting to go into town.
Once in the city, she saw a big ball of fluff coming up the street,
and she thinks to herself, "This thing looks pretty neat!"

"Bon Jour," said this fluffy thing,
"My name is Fifi and I come from Paris, which is in France,
where we love to doodle, prance and dance."

She continued, "France is my country, which is on the European continent -
our countryside and our city are both very pretty!
In Paris, *Qui* means *Yes* and we care about the way we dress.
We like to meet at the café,
and Bonjour is how we say, Good day!"
Fifi has HOPE that everyone will learn to
encourage freedom of expression
by sharing in art, food and fashion!

Nellie and Fifi notice we all have different likes and fancies.
Each of us is unique.
We are ALL sometimes bold and sometimes meek.
They both decided to take a chance,
and they realized in a glance,
when we join together in the dance of life,
we can ALL help each other and ease some strife.

Happily they sing, "We are ALL unique – Ces't magnifique!"
"WE are ALL different, but WE are ALL the same!"

There came along a tall, distinguished looking dog
with ears super long and howling like a song.
He has so much hair, Nellie can't see if he is smiling under there.
His hair is like a shaggy rug,
and Nellie is uncertain if she can give him a hug.

"I am Ali from Afghanistan, which is in the middle-east on the
continent of Asia," he explained, "You may be contemplating
why is my coat is so very long and what is my peculiar song?"
Nellie wants to learn more about Ali and the middle-east.
So he shared with her about his home,
and even though he likes to roam,
Ali is always welcome back to their beautiful feast!

He tells Nellie, "My coat is actually hair to keep me protected
from the sun, wind and sand.
It is very hot and dry in my native land."
This dog with an extra shaggy coat likes to sing, jump
and swim in a moat.

Ali continued, "I howl and sing to share HOPE through music in
every land, a wonderful song of peace from shore to sand.
I believe we can ALL walk together and live hand in hand!"

These two new friends connected that day
as they shared a fun time learning and at play!
Nellie and Ali were both thankful to make a new friend, you see,
each of us wants to be happy and free!

So united and in unison they sang -
"We are ALL different, but WE are ALL the same!"

Nellie learns to find HOPE on her journey, each and every day,
whether she is happy or sad, when at work or at play!

It is very important to care about our wonderful world in which we all share.
There are 7 continents on our beautiful planet earth
and billions of dogs, people and creatures —
WE are ALL students and WE are ALL teachers!

Nellie meets dogs and makes friends galore,
And she is excited to meet even more!
From the north, south, east and west — up and down,
even right here in her own home town!

Nellie has learned that no two are alike;
WE are ALL so different in so many ways,
Yet, WE ALL need the same things ALL of our days!
WE are ALL different in the way we look, bark and wag our tails,
Some are fast as lightning, some are slow as snails!
Nellie discovers she can help others,
and WE are ALL sisters and brothers!

WE ALL need to nourish our mind, body and mood,
with love, kindness, acceptance and a joyful attitude!

So as you go through your day,
and meet and greet others on your way...
Please think about how LOVE makes the world go 'round and 'round,
and the funny swooshing tail of Nellie Goldie Gray!

Remember to laugh and find HOPE each and every day,
and please don't be afraid to happily exclaim –
"WE are ALL different, but WE are ALL the same!"

Teacher Study Guide:

Book Title: "WE are ALL different, but WE are ALL the same!"

From the Tails of Nellie Goldie Gray book series.

Author: Tina Sweeney

Morals: Acceptance, Anti-bullying, Inclusion, Equality, Love

Social Studies: "SEE, THINK & WONDER"

Discuss and identify the social aspects and interactions throughout the story. The story promotes: friendship, love, serving, sharing, playing, caring and inviting others.

Geography:

Students learn and can name the seven continents.
For fun: match the dogs to the continents they come from.
Extra Challenge Activity: Identify the country each dog comes from and the name of breed.

Bonus Activities:

Look for and find HOPE the butterfly throughout the book. Lead a discussion about the virtue of HOPE, what HOPE means and how we can always find HOPE in every day.
Counting — Count backwards from 10 – 1.
Find the dog that is "different" on the last page of the book.

VOCABULARY:

1. Acquaintance - a person's knowledge or experience of something
2. Commotion - a confused and noisy disturbance
3. Compassion - pity and concern for others
4. Contemplate - think about something for a long time
5. Continent - one of several large land masses
6. Dainty - delicately small and pretty
7. Distinguished - successful, authoritative, and commending great respect
8. Echoing - repeated sound after the original sound has stopped
9. Encourage - give support, confidence or hope to someone
10. Fascinated - strongly attracted and interested
11. Frolicking – play cheerfully, excitedly, or energetically
12. Hue - a gradation or variety of a color; tint.
13. Isle - a small island
14. Moat a deep, wide trench filled with water, surrounding a town or castle
15. Mysterious - of a puzzling nature; inexplicable
16. Notion - vague or imperfect concept or idea
17. Ponder - to consider something deeply and carefully in the mind
18. Precise - being exact or definite
19. Rambunctious - difficult to control or handle; wildly boisterous
20. Resemble - to be alike or similar to
21. Similar - having a likeness or resemblance; especially in a general way
22. Suspect - to doubt or mistrust
23. Unfamiliar - different, unusual, unaccustomed, strange
24. Unison - when all elements behave in the same way at the same time (Example: singing)
25. Ventured - dare to enter or go, take a risk; to make or embark on an adventure
26. Wise - aware of right and wrong; having knowledge as to facts and circumstances.

Printed in the United States
by Baker & Taylor Publisher Services